Thanks to Phoenix and Scout
for giving me their love.
WH

Allanté, your paw prints
can be seen in the stars
as well as on our hearts.
SW

Library of Congress Cataloging-in-Publication Data
Hanson, Warren.
  Paw prints in the stars : a farewell and journal for a beloved pet /
written and illustrated by Warren Hanson.
    p. cm.
  ISBN 978-0-931674-89-1
  1. Pet loss—-Poetry. I. Title.
  PS3558.A54378P39 2008
  811'.54—-dc22

2008027368

TRISTAN Publishing, Inc.
2355 Louisiana Avenue North
Golden Valley, MN 55427

Please visit us at:
www.tristanpublishing.com

PAW PRINTS *in the* STARS

A Farewell and Journal
for a Beloved Pet

written and illustrated by
WARREN HANSON

TRISTAN PUBLISHING
Minneapolis

I will always know you loved me.

But it's time for me to go.

I was your soulmate, your companion,

and your friend.

We meant more to one another

than the world will ever know.

We were devoted to each other

to the end.

So when you find that you are missing me,

just listen to your heart,

and you will know that

I am never very far.

Each time you stand beneath the heavens,

and look up to face the dark,

you will see my shining paw prints

in the stars.

We loved each other from the start.

I found a home inside your heart

because you opened it so wide

to welcome me.

I hope you hold me there forever,

even when we are apart.

There's no place on earth

where I would rather be.

We were wonderful together.

Nothing else felt quite as right

as lying quietly

beneath your loving hand.

Sharing nibbles in the kitchen.

Sharing cuddles in the night.

Little rituals we grew to understand.

I have waited at the window,

hoping you would be home soon,

and I was glad when you would

greet me at the door.

I loved sleeping in the sunshine

of a winter afternoon,

just a happy heap of fur upon the floor.

We have learned from one another.

We have shared the precious lessons

we would not have gotten if we were alone.

And those lessons we have learned

have each been turned into a blessing.

And with every blessing,

our two hearts have grown.

We've both learned patience, trust, and loyalty.

We've both learned to forgive.

We've learned that happiness

can be a simple thing.

The little pleasures are the ones

that have the greatest gifts to give.

A wooden stick, a rubber ball,

a piece of string.

My water dish, my toys, my bed —

the simple things I leave behind —

they may remind you that

you miss me every day.

So if you want to put them out of sight,

I really wouldn't mind.

It doesn't mean our love

is being put away.

It's all right that you have spoiled me,

fed me treats I didn't need

so I would try the tricks

you wanted me to learn.

And, yes, I guess I slept in bed with you

a time or two. But then,

it gave me joy to give you

something in return.

I gave you comfort and companionship.

You've never felt alone,

because you knew that I was

somewhere in the house.

I gave you someone you could count on.

When you needed me,

you've known that I'd be there,

and there were never any doubts.

And now you know that I am somewhere else.

A place of perfect peace.

A happy home, where angels wait,

above the blue.

If you and I won't be together,

this is where I want to be,

with love forever,

like the love I had with you.

I will always know you loved me.

But it's time to say goodbye.

I was your soulmate, your companion,

and your friend.

Now I am free to play forever

in that place beyond the sky.

A happy paradise,

where life will never end.

So when you find that you are missing me,

just listen to your heart,

and you will know that

I am never very far.

Each time you stand beneath the heavens,

and look up to face the dark,

you will see my shining paw prints

in the stars.